For Peewee

First published in Great Britain by Hutchinson,
an imprint of Random House Children's Books, 2006
Printed and bound in China
First American edition, 2006
1 3 5 7 9 10 8 6 4 2

www.fsgkidsbooks.com

Library of Congress Cataloging-in-Publication Data
Deacon, Alexis.
   While you are sleeping / Alexis Deacon.— 1st American ed.
     p. cm.
   Summary: A girl's bedside toys go to great lengths to keep her
safe at night while she is asleep.
   ISBN-13: 978-0-374-38330-5
   ISBN-10: 0-374-38330-8
   [1. Toys—Fiction. 2. Night—Fiction. 3. Sleep—Fiction.]
I. Title.

PZ7.D33923 Whi 2006
[E]—dc22
                                 2005054168

While You Are Sleeping

Alexis Deacon

FARRAR, STRAUS AND GIROUX / NEW YORK

We are the bedside toys.

Do you ever stop to think what we go through,
night after night, to look after you?

All day we sit as still as stone,

waiting,   waiting,   waiting.

But when the sun goes down
and we're absolutely *sure* you're sleeping . . .

. . . we get up.
We shake our heads.
We stretch our weary legs.
"Another long night
ahead," we say.

But what's this?
A new toy?

He'll have to help us with our work
if he wants to join our crew.

Each night the whole room
must be checked.

Every cupboard.

Every corner.

We even peek behind the curtains,

and, if we're feeling brave,

underneath the bed.

But we can't stay long.
There's lots more work for us to do!

If you're too hot,

too cold,

or ill . . .

we try to make it better.

Bedbugs won't   bite. We squish them flat.

We scare
bad dreams away.

And on that one night
when you absolutely must not wake,
we make sure you don't.

We keep you safe no matter what.
That's our job, you see.

If you need us . . .

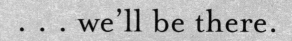

. . . we'll be there.

And when the sun comes up,
we use our last bit of strength
to crawl back to our places.

Just in time!

Why do we do it?
Why do we put ourselves through it,
night after night after night?
The new toy knows the answer . . .

Now he's a bedside toy, too.